LaLa Feels Blah Blah La

Teia Kayne
Goran Vitanovic

You are now entering..

LaLa wakes up feeling rotten, but she's not sure why. She's not sick, and the sun is shining.

LaLa feels Blah-la.

She
stomps
downstairs
for breakfast.

Stomp. Stomp. Stomp.

Mom is cheery and sings, "Good morning LaLa!" with a bright smile.

"Are you blue?"
Mom asks gently.

"No! I'm skin-colored, like always.

It's just a bad day.

An icky day!

An 'I don't know why I feel bad, but I do' kind of day."

"Well," says Mom, "why don't we try and make the day better with a happy breakfast?"

"I hate breakfast."

"Then I'll make you a happy lunch!"

Mom is not giving up.

"Okay." Mom shrugs.

"Why are you so happy any way, Mom?"

"That's a great question, LaLa! What you let yourself think will become your reality.

So, every time I start to feel icky, I think of a happy thought and everything changes!

Why don't you try it?"

LaLa shakes her head. "Don't want to."

"Just once?" Mom pleads as she hugs LaLa's shoulders.

"Close your eyes,
take a deep breath and

imagine a coin.

Right now it's on tails which is bad and BLAH feelings.

Imagine flipping that coin over to heads, which is joyful and happy feelings."

LaLa starts to smile and opens her eyes.
She pulls her plate towards her and
starts to eat her happy pancake.

"You know what, Mom?"

"What, LaLa?"

"I'm going to make

today a happy day!"

About LaLa's World

As a spiritually centered mom of four who is committed to natural living, I was inspired to write LaLa's World after over a decade of reading countless popular children's books and realizing that only a handful of stories truly serve to impart spiritual wisdom. My intention with this series is to help my daughters and other children better understand how their beliefs manifest their realities so they can grow up to be the change they wish to see in the world.

For my world, Joshua, Britton, Laurel, Maisie and Arya

Published in the United States by Inspired Content, a division of The Virtue Agency.
Visit us online! VirtueAgency.com

LaLa Feels Blah-La / Tela Kayne. — 1st Edition
Illustrated by Goran Vitanovic
Summary: LaLa wakes up feeling blah and her mom teaches her to turn her mood around with the flip of a coin.

Library of Congress Control Number: 2018904701
ISBN 13 978-0-692-07296-7 (hardcover)
ISBN 13 978-1-7321980-0-5 (kindle)
ISBN: 978-1-9808669-6-1 (KDP)

Discover LaLas.World

Made in the USA
Middletown, DE
14 September 2018